Ask for May, Settle for June

Doonesbury books by G. B. Trudeau

Still a Few Bugs in the System
The President Is a Lot Smarter Than You Think
But This War Had Such Promise
Call Me When You Find America
Guilty, Guilty, Guilty!
"What Do We Have for the Witnesses, Johnnie?"
Dare To Be Great, Ms. Caucus
Wouldn't a Gremlin Have Been More Sensible?
"Speaking of Inalienable Rights, Amy..."
You're Never Too Old for Nuts and Berries
An Especially Tricky People
As the Kid Goes for Broke
Stalking the Perfect Tan
"Any Grooming Hints for Your Fans, Rollie?"
But the Pension Fund Was Just Sitting There
We're Not Out of the Woods Yet
A Tad Overweight, but Violet Eyes to Die For
And That's My Final Offer!
He's Never Heard of You, Either
In Search of Reagan's Brain
Ask for May, Settle for June

In Large Format

The Doonesbury Chronicles
Doonesbury's Greatest Hits
The People's Doonesbury

a Doonesbury book by

GB Trudeau.

Ask for May, Settle for June

An Owl Book   Holt, Rinehart and Winston / New York

Published by Holt, Rinehart and Winston,
383 Madison Avenue, New York, New York 10017.

Published simultaneously in Canada by Holt, Rinehart and
Winston of Canada, Limited.

Library of Congress Catalog Card Number: 81-84328

ISBN Hardbound: 0-03-061532-1
ISBN Paperback: 0-03-061522-4

First Edition

Printed in the United States of America

The cartoons in this book have appeared in newspapers
in the United States and abroad under the auspices of
Universal Press Syndicate.

2 4 6 8 10 9 7 5 3 1

ISBN 0-03-061532-1 HARDBOUND

ISBN 0-03-061522-4 PAPERBACK